Never Were Men So Brave

Also by Susan Provost Beller
TO HOLD THIS GROUND:
A Desperate Battle at Gettysburg
(Margaret K. McElderry Books)

Never Were Men So Brave

THE IRISH BRIGADE DURING THE CIVIL WAR

SUSAN PROVOST BELLER

Illustrated with
thirty black-and-white drawings and photographs
and two maps

MARGARET K. McELDERRY BOOKS

Margaret K. McElderry Books

An imprint of Simon & Schuster Children's Publishing Division

1230 Avenue of the Americas

New York, New York 10020

Copyright © 1998 by Susan Provost Beller

Designed by Virginia Pope

Maps prepared by Rick Britton

The text of this book is set in Centaur

Printed in the United States of America

First Edition

10 9 8 7 6 5 4 3 2 1

Library of Congress Cataloging-in-Publication Data

Beller, Susan Provost, 1949-

Never were men so brave : the Irish Brigade during the Civil War/

Susan Provost Beller. — 1st ed.

p.   cm.

Includes bibliographical references (p.) and index.

Summary: Discusses the conditions in Ireland that led many to come to America in the mid-1800s, the
formation of the Union Army's Irish Brigade, and the experiences of these soldiers during the Civil War.

ISBN 0-689-81406-2

1. United States. Army of the Potomac. Irish Brigade—Juvenile literature. 2. United States—History—
Civil War, 1861-1865—Participation, Irish American—Juvenile literature. 3. Irish
Americans—History—19th century—Juvenile literature. [1. United States. Army of the Potomac. Irish
Brigade. 2. United States—History—Civil War, 1861-1865—Participation, Irish American. 3. Irish
American History—19th century.] I. Title.

E493.5I683B45 1998

973.7'41—dc21   97-16005

This book is
dedicated to
all of my husband's
Irish ancestors
Breen
Conlon
Lyons
Murphy
and
O'Brien
who came to America
but never lost
their love for
IRELAND

ACKNOWLEDGMENTS

My thanks for this book go first to my husband, W. Michael Beller, not only for his willingness to share his knowledge of the Civil War on demand, his tolerance for reading manuscripts, and his great photography, but also for his patience as I stood transfixed in Bloody Lane or talked to half the people in Ireland trying to capture how they feel about their history!

I am also grateful to all the people in Ireland, including those whose names I don't even know, for their willingness to talk about their country and its past. Everyone had a story to tell—a woman running a bed-and-breakfast who talked about how many Irish are forced to emigrate to work in the United Kingdom today, but then come home to retire; a tour guide at Kilmainham Gaol who talked about the effectiveness of the 1848 Rebellion; the schoolchildren in the town of The Commons who, fascinated by these strangers copying down the words on a monument they see every day, just had to tell the story as they are taught it at school and point out the "Warhouse" (the site of the Battle of Ballingarry) on the top of the distant hill; a bartender at a pub in Dublin, making the point of how "eight hundred years of English oppression" had affected how the Irish view authority today; a cousin of my husband's, Jeremiah Lyne, who was eager to show me the path taken by his grandfather to obtain the grass needed to feed the family's animals from the large fields declared off-limits by the English landowner. I've no doubt I could write ten books about the oppression of the Irish just from the stories shared by people throughout the country.

More specific thanks for photographic assistance to the Prints and Photographs Division of the Library of Congress; Michael Winey, of the United States Army Military History Institute; Donall O'Luanaigh, Keeper of Collections for the National Library of Ireland; Stuart O'Seanoir, Manuscripts Department of Trinity College Library, Dublin; Niamh O'Sullivan, Archivist for Kilmainham Gaol National Monument; and Kevin Harris for his assistance in preparing the contemporary pictures.

Thanks also go to Tim O'Reilly for reading the manuscript at an early stage. At a point where my original Antietam story was being taken over by the Irish story, his comments convinced me that I was right to head in that direction.

My thanks to Rick Britton for turning my sketches into his always wonderful maps and for checking to make sure I stay historically accurate.

Finally, my thanks, as always, to my editor, Emma D. Dryden, who makes sure I don't forget that my readers don't know as much about the Civil War as I do!

TABLE OF CONTENTS

PREFACE

On September 17, 1862, two armies made up of American soldiers met in a field by a creek in a small Maryland town in the middle of the Civil War—the bloodiest war ever fought in American history. The Union and Confederate armies that fought that day in Sharpsburg near Antietam Creek would leave behind a terrible record—a record of death that has not been equaled since. On that field, in the battle known to history as Antietam, lay the largest number of killed or wounded American soldiers ever to fall in one day's battle in our entire history. Over 23,700 Union and Confederate soldiers lay on the battlefield. No other bloody day of battles, not even those battles of World War II in which far greater numbers of soldiers fought, has ever matched this record of death set in September 1862.

The battle at Antietam began with a slaughter in the Cornfield and progressed to horrible fighting in the Sunken Road, which from this day on would be known as Bloody Lane, and finally to the bridge over the Antietam Creek, where unit after unit of Union soldiers tried to dislodge the Confederate troops holding this key position. In the Sunken Road alone over four thousand soldiers fell in three short hours of fighting. Over the several days following the battle, the dead were buried and both armies moved on to continue their fighting elsewhere. When the war finally ended three years later and our nation became one again, the hastily buried dead were moved into more permanent graves. Many bodies were never identified. Many missing soldiers were never found and could not be buried properly in marked graves.

In 1988, some Civil War souvenir hunters found a shallow grave in a Maryland farmer's field near the area of Bloody Lane. Buried in the grave were the remains of four soldiers. The remains of three of the men were very incomplete—just bits of bone and teeth. But the fourth man was different. It was possible to tell that he had died from the three Confederate bullets in his chest. His rosary was still around his neck, and there were enough clues such as uniform buttons and pieces of equipment to identify him as a member of the famous Irish Brigade. In the words of one historian, the Irish Brigade was known "for the recklessness of their charges and their tenacity under fire." Stephen Potter, National Park Service archaeologist, began a search to try to identify the soldier and finally narrowed down the possibilities to three members of the Irish Brigade who died in the fighting at Bloody Lane. Beyond that, it was impossible to say who the man was.

But in many ways it didn't really matter. Five hundred thirty-five members of the Irish Brigade were killed or wounded during their heroic charge into the Confederate lines at Antietam. The story of this one soldier was only a small part of the story of all the brave men of Irish descent who made up one of the most famous units of the Union army during the Civil War.

Here is their story....

Irish Brigade dead from the Battle of Antietam, September 1862

CHAPTER 1:

Their Mother, Ireland

It was the spring of 1863. Though weakened by their heroic deeds and heavy losses at Antietam and Fredericksburg, the Irish Brigade was ready for the fighting to begin again. One can imagine the thoughts of these soldiers turning to those at home, to their comrades lost, to the horrors of war ahead. But not the soldiers of the Irish Brigade—they were more concerned with something happening three thousand miles away, across the Atlantic Ocean, in Ireland. For these men, many of whom had left Ireland themselves because of a great famine, the needs of their distant brothers were very much on their minds, and they dug deep in their pockets to send whatever money they had.

Father William Corby, a chaplain of the Irish Brigade, included in his memoirs a letter he sent to the Archbishop of New York in May 1863 along with $1240.50 he had collected from the officers and men of the brigade for "the relief of the suffering poor in Ireland." A list of the men and their donations followed— donations of $1, $2, $5, even $10—enormous sums of money for men earning only $13 a month and needing that money themselves to support their families at home.

Father Corby apologized to the archbishop for the small amount donated, noting that "the amount would have been far greater had not our ranks been so horribly thinned by deaths, wounds, and sickness." Then he wrote of "that noble charity and love of country, which has, and I hope ever will, characterize the Irish emigrant in America." Love of country, indeed! Why were these Irish people so loyal to their mother country across the ocean when their new home in America had given them so much more?

Many of the Irish who came to America in the 1800s faced hard choices in Ireland: to stay in Ireland and starve, or to leave their families and friends to go to America and be able to have food to eat and a future for themselves and their families. Although Ireland was a beautiful land and their home, it was also a harsh land, filled with bogs and rocky hills, ill-suited to farming. Today the ruins of old houses litter the landscape in many areas, reminding the visitor of what sent so many Irishmen across the sea to America, Canada, or Australia in the late 1840s.

Ireland had been under English domination since the 1100s; but it was the Irish loss to the English at the Battle of the Boyne in July 1690 that made life miserable for the Catholic Irish. The problems that would drive them from their homes during the famine of the 1800s began when the English imposed rules known as the Penal Laws. The English were determined to stop the Irish from their periodic rebellions by taking away their culture and Catholic religion and by making them totally dependent on the English for economic survival.

The Anglo Irish, Protestant descendants of the original

English conquerors, owned about 80 percent of the land and rented it out to tenant farmers—the native Catholic Irish, who made up three quarters of the population of Ireland. The tenant farmers paid the rent to their landlords with the oats and barley that they grew and the animals that they raised. They used whatever was left over to feed their families. The miracle crop for the tenant farmers was the potato. On only an acre and a half of land, enough potatoes could be grown to feed a large family. It was a boring diet, but historians estimate that about half of the eight million people living in Ireland in the 1840s lived only on potatoes. As long as the crop was good most years, the farmers and their families survived.

Under the Penal Laws, Catholics were not allowed to be members of any of the professions, like law or teaching, although some were allowed to become doctors. Catholics could not own businesses. They couldn't even own a horse that was worth more than five pounds (about five to ten dollars). Catholics were forced to divide their land among all of their sons instead of being able to have the eldest son inherit the entire property and keep the farm intact. And Catholics could not legally buy or sell land without becoming Protestants. These economic laws made it impossible for the Catholic Irish to support themselves and made them more and more dependent upon their Protestant landlords, who wanted the Catholics to fail as farmers so that they could take their land and make their own estates larger. Irish Catholic families were forced to send their children into the fields of their Protestant landlords at night to steal grass to feed the family's animals. Without the animals, they would be unable to pay the rent on their farms. But, as bad as these economic laws were, what made the people most angry were the other provisions of the Penal Laws.

The Catholic Irish were forbidden to practice their religion or to teach it to their children. Irish Catholic priests were forbidden from celebrating Mass for their parishioners. There was not much the Irish could do about the economic laws, but they fought back against the suppression of their religion by practicing it in secret. Today one can visit the townland of Altar in County Cork, named for the three-thousand-year-old Stone Age wedge tomb where, during the time of the Penal Laws, a priest would celebrate Mass for the local Catholics using the flat top of the tomb as his altar. Catholic parents would have their children gather in small groups called "hedge schools" to learn to read and to learn about their religion. The children had small catechisms from which to learn. Because it was illegal for Catholics to own books or to be educated about Catholicism, the children learned to sit on the catechisms to hide them if someone came by.

The Catholic Irish were especially devoted to praying on their rosary beads. Like the dead soldier found at Antietam, they would always carry their rosary with them. But the forbidden rosaries, with their fifty-nine beads to mark the "Hail, Mary" and other prayers, were too long. Someone came up with a small rosary, called the An Paidrín Beag, which could be worn like a simple bracelet. The shorter rosary allowed the Catholics to say their prayers without the risk of being punished.

By the early 1800s the Irish Parliament, with permission of the English government, repealed some of the worst of the Penal Laws. But the years of English oppression could not be easily remedied. John Mitchel, a newspaperman who would later be imprisoned for his writings, wrote: "The Irish people were impoverished and debased. And so the English, having forbidden them for generations

Irish Stone Age wedge tomb used as an altar for saying Mass during suppression of the Catholic religion in the 1700s.

W. Michael Beller

to go to school, became entitled to taunt them with ignorance; and having deprived them of lands, and goods, and trade, magnanimously mock their poverty." To this "impoverished and debased" people who were just barely surviving, 1845 brought a nightmare. Potato crops throughout Ireland were attacked by a disease called a blight. The potatoes seemed fine when they were picked, but within days they rotted and could not be eaten. The disease reappeared the following year, and again the following three years. The Great Potato Famine, sometimes called "The Great Hunger," left the people of Ireland without food and without money to pay their rent and taxes. Over one million Irish died of hunger or diseases caused by the famine.

The English government did not know how to respond to this disaster. The existing laws allowed for poor relief only after the tenant farmer signed away his land to the landlord. The landlords paid "rates" (taxes) on the number of people actually living on their property and on any tenants who went to the workhouses for relief. As the famine worsened and the tenants were unable to pay their rent to the landlords, the landlords had no money to pay the rates. The only way the landlords could stop paying rates on the tenants was to tear their houses down and force them off the property. So the starving Irish families who had signed over their land because they could not pay the rent were now evicted from the land. Teams of horses were brought in and the vacated houses were literally torn down and their hearths plowed. People were forced to live in ditches. Whole villages disappeared.

Some people were allowed into the workhouses, which were run on the principle that "Relief should be made so unattractive as to furnish no motive to ask for it except in the absence of every other means of subsistence." But since so many people had no choice but to go to the workhouses, they quickly filled up. The evicted families that were turned away from the workhouses had nowhere to go and nothing to eat. Many ate grass and raw shellfish, and finally died of starvation and disease.

What most angered those fighting for the rights of the Catholic Irish was that there was plenty of food available in Ireland during the famine years. John Mitchel pointed out that during the worst years of the famine (1845–48), "Ireland was exporting to England food to the value of fifteen million pounds sterling, and had on her own soil at each harvest, good and ample provision for double her own population, notwithstanding the potato blight."

Other nations sent ships full of food to help the Irish who were starving. The English government made some token efforts to provide aid and appointed groups to study the situation. But no one took action to repeal the laws that drove the Irish from their small farms and gave them only the option of staying and possibly starving, or emigrating. Places like America and Australia began to look like good opportunities. Especially America. Historian Ian Gibson wrote: "Most Irish who came probably didn't know much about America. But they knew America had gotten rid of the British, and that must have been a great comfort."

One historian wrote that the Irish saw themselves as "unhappy exiles." They were glad to be in America, but they did not feel that they had come by choice. For many of them, Ireland remained their real home. They did all they could to send money home to help those still left behind in their homeland. Many of the Irish in America also harbored a dream of someday returning to Ireland and taking it by force from the English, creating their own Irish nation. For the Irish in America, Ireland was their mother indeed.

By 1848, within three years of the beginning of the famine, Ireland had lost two million of her eight million people either to starvation or emigration. Wrote one historian: "No country ravaged by a hostile army could have been reduced to a more deplorable condition."

CHAPTER 2:

Young Ireland and the Rebellion of 1848

There was a small group of Catholic Irish who had managed to become moderately successful and made enough money to send their sons out of the country so they could receive a Catholic education. These wealthier, better-educated Irish were trying to work to improve conditions and allow the Irish to gain greater control over their own country. Leading the Catholic Irish fighting to achieve political and religious freedom was the great politician Daniel O'Connell, who, after his election to the English Parliament, had been working toward a political solution to these issues. His hope was for some independence from England now; and, over the very long term, a fully independent Ireland. Although some progress had been made, the hardships of the famine had made many Irish feel that bold and decisive action was required immediately.

Young Thomas Francis Meagher (pronounced MARR) admired and respected O'Connell. In September 1843, at the age of twenty, Meagher had made his first political speech at a rally and had been congratulated by O'Connell with the words "Well done,

Thomas Francis Meagher at the time of the speech that gained him the nickname "Meagher of the Sword." *Library of Congress*

Young Ireland." But Meagher and the other younger Irish leaders increasingly came to feel that O'Connell's way of solving Ireland's problems was too slow, and the name "Young Ireland" came to symbolize their whole cause.

After a speech he gave in Dublin in 1846 in which he publicly criticized the Repeal Association that was headed by O'Connell, Meagher earned a new nickname, "Meagher of the Sword." Meagher's speech criticized the Repeal Association's policy that force should never be used in the fight for Irish independence. Recalling the success of the American Revolution in 1776, where force had earned America independence from England, Meagher would not rule out the need for force to achieve Irish independence: "I do not abhor the use of arms in the vindication of national rights. There are times when arms will alone suffice, and when political ameliorations call for a drop of blood, and many thousand drops of blood." Meagher's speech was a powerful one, and the leaders of the Repeal Association did not give him a chance to finish it. In protest, he and the other members of the Young Ireland movement walked out of the meeting.

For two years following that meeting, "Meagher of the Sword" and the other leaders of Young Ireland made themselves into a nuisance for the local Anglo Irish authorities with their fiery speeches and newspaper articles. Finally the authorities decided to arrest a Young Ireland leader, Smith O'Brien, who was seen by many people as the future "king" of Ireland. Arrests of Meagher and other members of Young Ireland were also ordered. *The Times of London* rejoiced at the arrest orders. For Meagher and a Darcy McGee, the newspaper had no patience: "These gentlemen are free to spout treason without let or hindrance. They are beyond compassion, the two most dangerous men in connexion with the movement, the former especially, on account of his restless energy and that mastery of language which at once charms and frenzies an Irish mob to the commission of any enterprise, however desperate or hopeless." Gathered at the Widow McCormack's house (known today as the "Warhouse") in Ballingarry, the Young Ireland members decided to resist arrest and start a revolution.

On July 28, 1848, the leaders of the Young Ireland movement met for the last time at a place known now as The Commons. Today a monument marks the spot where "according to tradition the Tricolour was raised during the 1848 Rebellion." Upon the monument are the words of Thomas Francis Meagher as he presented the new flag of Ireland to the people. Meagher said: "The white of the centre signifies a lasting truce between the Orange and the Green and I trust that beneath its folds the hands of the Irish Protestant and the Irish Catholic may be clasped in generous and heroic brotherhood." The flag (which is the flag of the Republic of Ireland today) is made up of the three colors Meagher spoke of: orange, symbolizing the Protestant Orangemen; white; and green, symbolizing the native Catholic Irish. The flag flies over the monument continually today "in commemoration of its origins." But the truce Meagher hoped for was not to be.

The Times of London chronicled both the increasing tension in the countryside of Ireland and the final confrontation between the Young Ireland leaders and the police on July 29, 1848. "The rebellion, having actually commenced this morning on the common of Boulagh, near Ballingarry, has been decisively checked by the firmness and courage of fifty or sixty police. Three [actually one] of the insurgents have, I believe, paid the penalty of their rashness with

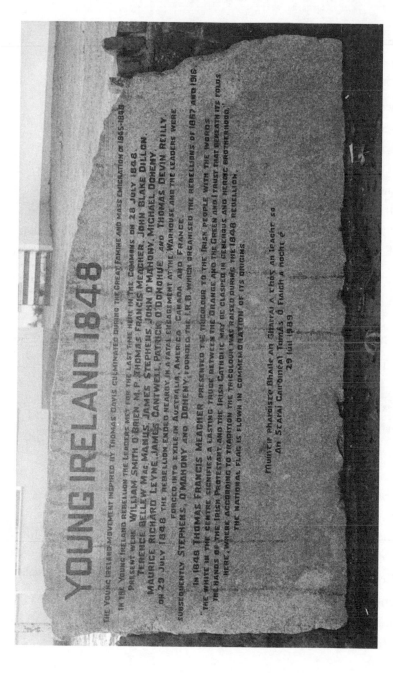

Young Ireland monument marking the spot where Thomas Francis Meagher presented the Irish flag to the people of Ireland in 1848.

W. Michael Beller

their lives, more are wounded," reported the correspondent in the August 1st edition of the paper.

By August 15th, *The Times of London* announced the arrest of Meagher and several others. The editors could not help but note of Meagher: "His appearance is not vulgar, but 'pretentious', and you see in it ...the usual characteristics of an *ad captandem* [publicity-seeking] orator." Of John Kavanagh, wounded in the incident at Ballingarry, *The Times* reported that he "had the good fortune to elude the vigilance of the police, although deeply implicated in the late abortive rebellion."

Meagher was the star of his own trial. Accused of treasonous speeches and inciting the population to revolt, even the English prosecutor commented on his eloquence and popularity. *The Times* quoted the prosecutor as saying: "The youth and personal attributes of Mr. Meagher, his eloquence and misguided ability all combine to render him an especial favorite with such a people as the Irish, who are more readily influenced by their feelings than by their judgment." These sorts of prejudices about the Irish people were very typical of the English press at that time. *The Times* reported also that "the prisoner had frequent demands for autographs."

Meagher himself showed his public speaking ability with his presentencing speech: "I am here to regret nothing I have ever done—to retract nothing I have ever spoken. I am here to crave with no lying lips the life I consecrate to the liberty of my country." His popularity and eloquence would not save him from being found guilty, however. Along with the others involved in the 1848 Rebellion, he was given the normal sentence for treason; he was to be "hanged, drawn and quartered," a particularly brutal form of execution. But the judges also made "a unanimous recommendation of mercy for the prisoner's youth."

Meagher and Smith O'Brien while prisoners at Kilmainham Gaol, Dublin

Kilmainham Gaol and Museum

A form of "mercy" was granted, and Meagher and the other Young Ireland leaders were sentenced to house arrest and exile in Van Diemen's Land (now called Tasmania), an island off the coast of Australia. Their imprisonment was not harsh. As long as they gave their "parole," or word, that they would not attempt to escape, they would be assigned to live in separate villages. Meagher was sent to Campbell Town, to live in a district thirty-five miles across by fifteen miles wide. Although the prisoners were not supposed to be in contact with each other, they did actually meet from time to time. John Mitchel, already imprisoned (for "treasonous" articles he wrote in a newspaper in the spring of 1848) by the time of the Young Ireland Rebellion, was taken from his English prison on the island of Bermuda and also placed in Van Diemen's Land. Mitchel wrote of his first meeting with Meagher and other Young Irelanders in April 1850: "It has pleased me well at any rate to find that my friends are all *unsubdued*. The game, I think, is not over yet." The men discussed the news that Irish refugees in America considered them to be "martyrs" to the cause of Irish independence. Mitchel wrote: "It seems I have my faction, and Meagher a still stronger one." If they could ever escape from their far-off island exile, perhaps their status as martyrs could be used to further the Irish cause.

Three years later, Meagher gave notice that he intended to violate his parole and escape. He sent a letter to the police magistrate on January 3, 1852, announcing that he was surrendering his "ticket of leave" effective on January 4th. The police magistrate immediately ordered his arrest. But the Chief of Police refused to arrest his fellow Irishman. By the time the English magistrate was able to make other arrangements to arrest Meagher, Meagher had left. He traveled to meet the fishing boat that would take him out to an island to wait for the ship that would give him his freedom. After a tense eight-day wait, the *Elizabeth Thompson* arrived, and Meagher traveled to Brazil where he boarded an American ship bound for New York. Mitchel would join him there in November 1853.

The ill-fated Young Ireland Rebellion, which the English sarcastically called the "Battle of Widow McCormack's Cabbage Patch," was a military failure. The battle was over and the war had been lost, or so it seemed. But for the Irish in America, it was a different story. In the Battle of Ballingarry, they saw a romantic attempt to gain Ireland's independence. One historian noted that Young Ireland's "cry for revolution and revenge inspired embittered ...Irish-Americans to their greatest efforts to free Ireland and wreak vengeance for the horrors they had seen and suffered."

Meagher could see why Young Ireland had failed: "The defeat of 1848 was not the defeat of a whole people. It was nothing more than the rout of a few peasants, hastily collected, badly armed, half-starved, and miserably clad...We who went to Tipperary did not put the question properly to the country—did not give the country a fair opportunity—did not adopt anything like the best means for evoking the heroism of the people, and bringing it into action."

Less than twenty years later, Meagher's continuing commitment to free Ireland would lead to the creation of the Irish Brigade. The Irish would fight again, this time to the benefit of their new homeland—America.

CHAPTER 3:

The Irish in America

Both the famine immigrants and the exiled leaders of the Irish Rebellion found a new home in America. For many of the poor, though, both their journey and their arrival was far from a dream come true. Most of the famine immigrants came to America in steerage class. Steerage class most often was just one big open space in the ship's hold, so crowded that each person had about two square feet of space. On many ships, the Irish were locked in and not allowed to come up on deck for the entire journey, which often lasted fifty days or more. Without fresh air, with food that was rotten and usually only half-cooked, and with dirty water to drink, it is not surprising that many people became sick and died from "ship fever." Typical was a ship called the *Larch*, which sailed from Sligo, Ireland. Of the original 440 passengers, 108 died while the ship was at sea, and another 150 of them were sick with ship fever by the time the trip ended.

The famine immigrants arrived in America to find that many Americans did not welcome them and their strong Catholic faith. A group of Americans called the "Know-Nothings" were anti-Catholic and tried to drive the Irish from their new homes. The Know-Nothings were strongest in Eastern cities such as New York and Boston, where many of the new immigrants were living. Most of the Know-Nothings worked through the political system, getting people elected who shared their views. But some of them tried more direct means to drive the Catholic Irish out of America. At one Catholic school in Providence, Rhode Island, the Know-Nothings surrounded a convent where some Irish Catholic nuns lived, determined to burn down the building with them inside. But the frightened Sisters of Mercy would not be driven away and the building survived.

Most of the poor Irish came over to work at very low-paying jobs. The women tended to become servants or work in the textile mills. The men were mostly unskilled laborers, doing much of the work that others found too "dirty" to do. As poor as they were, however, the Irish found America a place where they could find sufficient food, a place where they could practice their religion openly, and a place where they could create a better life for their children.

Thomas Francis Meagher did not face the same problems of other Irish immigrants. He was welcomed to New York as a hero. The *New York Herald* described the fanfare as he arrived and noted that he was a "fine, military looking young gentleman, stoutly built, handsome, and always a favorite with the ladies."

Like all the other immigrants to America, Meagher needed to find a way to support himself. But, being Meagher, it also had to be a way to further the Irish cause. At first he became a touring lecturer, sharing accounts of the 1848 Rebellion and his imprisonment and escape. In 1855 he qualified to practice law in New York State. However, he finally ended up becoming a journalist.

In April 1856 he founded a newspaper called the *Irish News*.

The newspaper was well received and gave Meagher a forum for keeping the Irish issue on the minds of Irish-Americans. The *Irish News* included news from "home," world news, obituaries and marriages of Irish-Americans, reviews of books about Ireland or written by Irishmen, and many letters and articles reminiscing about Ireland and discussing her problems.

Being the editor of the paper and a prominent orator gave Meagher a chance to see much of America. Some of the views he developed are interesting. For example, Meagher toured the South in 1856 and had many positive things to say about what he found there. "I could see none of the horrors that I had been taught to believe existed among them [Southerners]," he wrote in the newspaper. "I found a people sober, intelligent, high-minded, patriotic, and kind-hearted ... I saw no poverty."

The *Irish News* and its editor began to adopt a fairly strong Southern viewpoint as the national discussion over slavery and the rights of the Southern states to choose which national laws they would follow continued to grow louder and angrier. Meagher saw Southerners somewhat as revolutionaries, people attempting to break free from an oppressor just as the Irish were trying to achieve their own independence from England. Meagher was not alone in this view. Many of the Irish viewed the American situation the same way. Vocal Irishmen like Meagher would argue the Southern point of view right up until the war itself began at Fort Sumter in April 1861.

As war broke out, Thomas Francis Meagher found himself with a difficult decision to make. He really did support the Southern position, but he could not walk away from the country that had welcomed him and given him a new life. He, and many other Irish leaders, also found another opportunity in America. The

Irish needed trained military leaders if they were going to gain their independence from Britain. Meagher saw a practical reason for the Irish to fight for the Union (which everyone thought was sure to win quickly). "It is a moral certainty," wrote Meagher, "that many of our countrymen who enlist in this struggle for the maintenance of the Union will fall in the contest. But even so, I hold that if only one in ten of us come back when this war is over, the military experience gained by that one will be of more service in a fight for Ireland's freedom than would that of the entire ten as they are now."

Others had seen the same opportunity. Captain David Conyngham wrote: "Many a patriotic young Irishman wanted to learn the use of arms and the science of war, with the hope of one day turning them to practical use in his own country."

The Irish-Americans, like other groups of immigrants, and even some families, would be split by the war. One of the exiles of the 1848 Young Ireland Rebellion, John Mitchel, worked in the Confederate capital of Richmond, Virginia, as editor of the *Richmond Examiner*, and he remained there throughout the Civil War. Mitchel, safe in Richmond, would not have to face his old friend on the battlefield, but he would lose a son fighting for the Confederacy at Gettysburg. There were Irish regiments that fought for both the Union and the Confederacy. Like the Germans, French, Swedish, Mexicans, Italians, Russians, and other immigrant groups in America, most of the Irish (more than 150,000 in all) fought with the Union. For whichever side the Irish fought, they would be remembered most for their fearless courage and bravery. The Irish Brigade might be the one whose story you read here, but remember that there were many other Irishmen fighting, equally brave, but not as famous. One Irish unit from Louisiana that fought for the South had a company of troops, Company B, that began their service with one hundred men and ended with only two. Company A of the same regiment did better. They, at least, had three soldiers and an officer left by March 1865. The Irish of both sides were known, in the words of historian Bell Irvin Wiley, as "the most desperate and dependable of fighters."

When the final choice had to be made, most Irish immigrants chose to fight to preserve their new country. Peter Welch, who became a color sergeant (the person who carried the flag, or colors, of the regiment) in the Irish Brigade, spoke for all the Irish-Americans when he wrote to a relative in Ireland in June 1863: "America is Irlands refuge Irlands last hope. Destroy this republic and her hopes are blasted. If Irland is ever [to be] free the means to acomplish it must come from the shores of America."

Thomas Francis Meagher could not have agreed more. Speaking the same month in Boston, trying to "recruit up" the numbers of soldiers in the Irish Brigade to make up for their losses at Antietam and Fredericksburg, Meagher knew that the Irish owed a debt to their new country: "I will not appeal to the gratitude of Irishmen in this invocation to arms. I will not remind them that when they were driven from their own land, when their huts were pulled down or burned above their heads, when turned out by the roadside or into the ditches to die, when broken in fortunes, and when all hope was lost, the Irishmen came here and had a new life infused into them ... and found thousands to give them encouraging and sustaining hands."

CHAPTER 4:

The Irish Come Out Fighting

Knowing what we know now of the long four-year struggle that the Civil War became, it is hard to go back and imagine what people expected would happen when the Union and Confederate armies met in battle for the first time on July 21, 1861. With the election in November 1860 of Abraham Lincoln as President of the United States, the Southern states began seceding from the "union" of states formed by the United States Constitution in 1787.

The states that seceded organized themselves into the Confederate States of America. They elected their own president, Jefferson Davis. At his inauguration, President Davis had one wish—that President Lincoln would allow "peaceable relations with you [the United States], though we must part." But President Lincoln had a responsibility to preserve the union of states, and so, in both Washington, D.C., and in Richmond, Virginia, the leaders of both sides prepared for a battle—but not for a war.

Both presidents called for soldiers to enlist for a ninety-day period, which seemed a long enough time for one quick and decisive battle. Most Northerners expected that the Union would win this battle, and then the Union and Confederate leaders would negotiate a political settlement of their differences. Since nearly everyone assumed that the "war" would be very short, they also assumed that the ninety-day soldiers would have plenty of time to train and prepare for the one great battle. There also wasn't much concern about common uniforms and flags, or the organization of the two opposing armies.

This would be a great adventure, and the officers who organized regiments made the most of the opportunity. They designed fancy, sometimes impractical, uniforms for their soldiers, and beautiful flags. Some so admired the French soldiers in Algeria, called Zouaves, who wore brightly colored uniforms and had their own style of drilling, that they formed their own Zouave units. Each leader trained his troops to follow his own signals and commands. It was not a very organized army on either side.

On July 21, 1861, the two armies met in battle near the small town of Manassas, Virginia. Confederate President Jefferson Davis was actually at the battle. Union politicians and ladies of Washington society had come in their carriages with picnic lunches to watch the Union army defeat the Confederates. But the results of the battle were not what had been expected. The Union army, mixed in with all those carriages, was sent fleeing back to Washington in a terrible defeat for the Union. The ninety-day soldiers were sent home and the work of building armies that could fight a war began.

In the middle of the fighting on that summer day, one regiment of soldiers, the 69th New York, which included a unit called Meagher's Zouaves, stood out from the rest for its bravery under fire.

Bayonet charge of the 69th New York at the Battle of First Manassas, July 1861

Once the decision was made to support their new country, Irishmen who fought on both sides did so with great courage. They earned themselves a reputation for never giving up a position, even if everyone around them was fleeing. Even in this first battle at Manassas, when the Union troops fled back to Washington, D.C., in a disorganized rout, the 69th New York "left the field in good order, with colors flying."

"The standard-bearer of the green flag of the Sixty-ninth was shot down, but the flag was instantly raised again. The second man was shot, and a rebel tore the flag from his grasp. Exerting himself, he shot down the rebel, rescuing the flag, and seized a rebel color; but he was soon overpowered by numbers, and the trophy taken from him, besides being taken prisoner with his own flag. He had a concealed revolver, and shot the two men in charge of him, and captured a captain's sword and a prisoner." This description of the actions of a brave and reckless John D. Keefe of Meagher's Zouaves of the 69th New York at the Battle of First Manassas was only the first of many heroic accounts of the fearlessness of Irish soldiers in battle. Many soldiers of the 69th New York would reenlist when the ninety-day troops were sent home and new regiments were formed. They would become the core unit of what would be called the Irish Brigade.

Countless stories of individual heroism by Irish soldiers would accumulate over the course of the Civil War. Captain David Conyngham, later a staff officer of the Irish Brigade, wrote of Meagher's Zouaves at Manassas: "[They] suffered desperately, their red dress making them a conspicuous mark for the enemy. When Meagher's horse was torn from under him by a rifled cannon ball, he jumped up, waved his sword, and exclaimed, 'Boys! look at that flag [their regimental colors]—remember Ireland.'"

Proud of his fellow Irishmen, Captain Conyngham even collected comments by their opponents to add to his memoir. About Manassas, he quoted a Southern officer who described the Irish regiment as "a rock in the whirlpool rushing past them." This officer also observed that "the Irish fought like heroes."

A newspaper correspondent for *The World* described "the rush of the Sixty-ninth to the death-struggle...coats and knapsacks were thrown to either side, that nothing might impede their work."

But these gallant charges and this reckless determination also gave the Irish soldiers who fought with the 69th New York and with the Irish Brigade their horrible record of losses. At each of their major battles, they suffered a considerable number of dead and wounded. Over the course of their service to the Union cause, the Irish Brigade experienced an 85 percent casualty rate. One historian wrote that of the seven thousand or so men who fought in the Irish Brigade during the Civil War, only one thousand returned home without being wounded.

Captain Conyngham recorded the casualties for the 69th New York Regiment—150 at Manassas—and wrote a memorial to each of the slain officers, a memorial that never failed to mention the Irish home of each of the soldiers: "Lieutenant-Colonel Haggerty, a native of Glenswilly, County Donegal, and as fine a specimen of a Celt as Ireland could produce, fell shot through the heart; while beside him fell poor Costelloe, a recent arrival from Waterford, and a noble, amiable youth."

At Manassas, the Irish soldiers set the glorious but bloody pattern for the battles to come—the daring gallantry, the somewhat reckless charges, the long list of casualties. Orator-turned-soldier Thomas Francis Meagher spoke of the death of Haggerty and the others and, in doing so, spoke for all of those to follow them in death over the next four years. "They lie there in rich sunshine, discolored, and cold in death. All of them were from Ireland, and as the tide of life rushed out, the last thought that left their hearts was for the liberty of Ireland."

Officers of the 69th New York Regiment

CHAPTER 5:

The Irish Brigade
Is Formed

The Confederate victory at Manassas shocked the Union leaders. It also showed each side that this was not going to be a short war. Neither the North nor the South was really ready for what was to follow, and both sides moved quickly to prepare themselves for the long conflict to come.

Many changes were made by the military leaders on both sides. Common-color uniforms were established for each army so that the troops would not fire on soldiers from their own side during a battle. A new flag was designed for the Confederates to distinguish it from the Union's "stars and stripes." The new Confederate battle flag had white stars on crossed blue bars on a red field, and was known popularly as the "stars and bars." In addition to better transportation and communication systems, better medical facilities were prepared to handle the large number of casualties that came when large armies met in battle. Both sides needed to develop armies that were disciplined, professional, and committed to serving for the duration of the war. Ninety-day troops could not be used.

Their training was barely completed when it was time for them to return home.

The 69th New York, along with all the other short-term units, disbanded and returned home after Manassas. Thomas Francis Meagher now set himself a new goal. He wanted to form an Irish Brigade, an entire brigade of 2,500 men, all of Irish descent. Using his great skill at public speaking, he began recruiting soldiers in the areas where most of the Irish had settled. As Captain Conyngham recalled Meagher's efforts: "America had welcomed him into her bosom [after his escape from Australia]; he now stood beside her in her hour of need. His pen of light and his burning words fired many a brave heart to uphold the flag of the Union with its best blood."

Meagher's public-speaking skills were always at their best when he had a cause that he felt very passionate about, and his latest passion was the need to defend the Union. Recruiting in New York in August 1861, he spoke from the heart: "Never, I repeat it, was there a cause more sacred, nor one more just, nor one more urgent. I ask no Irishman to do that which I myself am not prepared to do. My heart, my arm, my life are pledged to the national cause, and to the last it will be my highest pride, as I conceive it to be my holiest duty and obligation, to share in its fortunes." His speeches, in the words of Captain Conyngham, "brought many a stalwart recruit to the ranks of the Irish Brigade."

Meagher's speeches also motivated those who would stay at home when the Irish Brigade went off to fight. Charmed by Meagher's words, the women of New York gathered to present the brigade with a fitting set of flags to use in battle. These were presented to the Irish Brigade at a public ceremony, and everyone was impressed with their beauty and workmanship. Most admired were the regimental flags "of a deep rich green, heavily fringed, having in the centre a richly embroidered Irish harp, with a sunburst above it and a wreath of shamrock beneath. Underneath, on a crimson scroll, in Irish characters, was the motto, 'They shall never retreat from the charge of lances.'" These were regimental flags, one for each of the regiments that would together make up the Irish Brigade: the 69th, 88th, and 63rd Regiments, New York State Volunteers. Over time the Brigade would grow to include the 29th Massachusetts Regiment as well. Other units would be part of the Irish Brigade at different times during the Civil War. But these three original regiments would remain the heart of the Irish Brigade. Of the original 2,500 men mustered into the Irish Brigade, over 500 were veterans of that first major battle at Manassas. They were ready to fight behind their new green flags, and to preserve the reputation they had earned in that battle.

The Catholic Church also did its part to make the departure of these Irishmen for war a memorable occasion. The flag presentation took place at the home of the Catholic Archbishop on Madison Avenue in New York City. The Archbishop of New York was out of the country, but he was represented by a spokesman who told the soldiers that the Archbishop "has confidence in the fidelity of the Irish soldiers, for history has told us that the Irish soldier has always done his duty at home and abroad. Whenever his services have been employed he has never been found wanting. He has always been faithful to the trusts confided to him."

After their fine send-off from New York City, the brigade was sent to Camp California, outside of Alexandria, Virginia, where they established winter quarters and began training for the battles to

The 69th New York parades through New York City on their way to war   *Massachusetts MOLLUS Collection, USAMHI*

come. President Lincoln himself commended Colonel Meagher "for his patriotism and devotion . . . and his services in enrolling such a fine body of men as the Irish Brigade." In February 1862, Thomas Francis Meagher—"the living presence of the Brigade all through its career," in the words of Captain W. F. Lyons—was named a brigadier general and given command of the Irish Brigade. The unit was ready to take its place in history.

CHAPTER 6:

Irishmen and Soldiers

The Irish Brigade would not only bring together many of the men who had proved their bravery with the 69th New York at Manassas; many of the people made famous during the Irish independence movement would become officers in the Irish Brigade as well.

Thomas Francis Meagher would be the most famous. This hero of the 1848 Young Ireland Rebellion, sentenced originally to be "hanged, drawn and quartered" by the British courts, was born in Waterford, Ireland, in 1823. He came from a relatively wealthy family and was educated at schools in both Ireland and Great Britain. His greatest ability was as an orator. Now, in the Civil War, he would be judged on his actions, not his words. In many ways, he became the heart of the Irish Brigade. In battle, he was right there in the front lines with his troops, often with the result of having his horse shot out from under him. Biographer Robert Athearn wrote that "Meagher made it a practice to be in a conspicuous position when exposed to enemy fire and . . . where the fight was the hottest." It was an unusual place to find a brigade commander and it made his men fanatically loyal to him.

Brigadier General Thomas Francis Meagher, Commander of the Irish Brigade

Massachusetts MOLLUS Collection, USAMHI

Another Young Ireland refugee, John Kavanagh, was born in Dublin around 1826. He married Nannie Frances Byrne in June 1847, but that didn't keep him from becoming an active member of the Young Ireland movement. Captain Conyngham described Kavanagh as "a devoted, zealous patriot ...ably sustained by the patriotic enthusiasm and deep affection of his devoted young wife." He was wounded in the fighting in the 1848 Rebellion and escaped to the United States. His wife and first child joined him there. When the Civil War began, he was proud "to serve under his friend and fellow-exile, General Meagher." At thirty-five years of age and the father of seven children, Kavanagh had every possible excuse to stay home and let others fight this war. But he was determined to fight to preserve his new country. He helped organize a regiment of New York Volunteers and then took the opportunity to transfer to the Irish Brigade. He would lead a company of soldiers into action under the Brigade's famous green flag on the field at Antietam.

David Power Conyngham was born in 1825 in Crohane, County Tipperary, in Ireland. Active in the Young Ireland movement, he was not important enough (or enough of a troublemaker) to be arrested in 1848. He came to America during the Civil War as a newspaper correspondent. At times he served on Meagher's staff and collected information for a book on the Irish Brigade. The book, *The Irish Brigade and Its Campaigns*, aimed to "give a true and impartial history" of the Brigade "with the sole desire of helping to rescue from obscurity the glorious military record we [the Irish] have earned in America."

Father William Corby became one of the most famous members of the Irish Brigade. This Irish-American was not even born in Ireland. His father was born in Ireland, but he was born in

Detroit, Michigan, in 1833. Father Corby was ordained a priest in 1860 and joined the Irish Brigade as one of its chaplains in 1861. No one could have known then that Corby would be more famous than any other chaplain serving with any of the Union or Confederate armies. Nor could anyone have foreseen that one day he would have a statue raised in his honor on the battlefield at Gettysburg. One historian wrote that "the camp of the Irish Brigade …became the spiritual center of Catholicism in the army and Father Corby its most important figure." Chaplain Corby later wrote a book called *Memoirs of Chaplain Life: Three Years with the Irish Brigade in the Army of the Potomac.* He wrote not to give the details of battles, but "to give a realistic account of every-day life in the army." Known for his bravery serving his soldiers under fire, Chaplain Corby shared all the hardships of the soldiers.

Three other Irishmen would lead the Irish Brigade later in the war. Colonel Robert Nugent was born in Kilkeel, County Down. He fought with the Irish Brigade in every one of its battles except Antietam, when he was ill and unable to fight. Even though he received a horrible wound at Fredericksburg, he came back to continue fighting with the brigade. James Kelly would also command the Irish Brigade later in the Civil War. Born in County Monaghan, he began his career with the 69th New York and although severely wounded at Antietam, stayed in the army throughout the war. James McGee, born in Cushendall, County Antrim, was a Young Irelander who, unlike Meagher, left Ireland voluntarily. Before the war he was a journalist at *The Irish American* in New York, a rival newspaper to Meagher's *Irish News.*

Many other Irish names could be listed on a roll of honor for Irish patriots who now defended their new country in the Irish

David Power Conyngham (seated second from the left), newspaper correspondent for the *New York Herald* with the Army of the Potomac.

Brigade. Shortly after he joined the Brigade in the fall of 1861, Father Corby spoke of his new parishioners as he got to know the officers and men he would be serving as chaplain. He wrote of Thomas Francis Meagher: "He was a great lover of his native land, and passionately opposed to its enemies; strong in his faith, which he never concealed...and, wherever he went he made himself known as a 'Catholic and an Irishman.'" Corby went on to speak of the leadership Meagher provided to his officers and of how he "drew around him, not a low, uneducated class, but rather refined and gentlemanly officers and men ...to join his standard." The men of the Irish Brigade were, Chaplain Corby said, "Christian soldiers— unique in character, unique in faith, unique in nationality; but ever brave and true."

The 69th New York at Sunday Mass while in camp

CHAPTER 7:

The Irish Brigade at War

By the time spring arrived in 1862, the Irish Brigade was ready to depart from their headquarters at Camp California. With the rest of the Union army of the Potomac, the Irish Brigade began the campaign to capture the Confederate capital in Richmond, Virginia. Camp conditions had deteriorated since the spring rains had come and turned the ground into a sea of mud. Chaplain William Corby remembered one amusing tale of the mud: "One day I saw an officer attempt to cross the street in front of my tent in Camp California. When he reached the center, his boots sank so deep in the tough clay that he was obliged to call a soldier to dig him out with a spade. Even then, as he attempted to pull out one leg the other would sink, and so on, till it became impossible for him to extricate himself except by pulling his feet out of his boots and escaping in his stocking feet."

Father Corby wrote his account of hardships in camp so that "the reader will understand that a soldier suffers a thousand times more from every-day hardships in war than from the simple fact of entering a battle-field, where, for a few hours, he is in the midst of bloody strife, and, perhaps, at last receives a flesh wound or drops to speak no more." The Irish Brigade was more than ready to trade the hardships of winter camp for the unknown hardships of the march. It would only take one day of walking eighteen miles through rain and mud, carrying their heavy knapsacks, to convince them that the boredom of living in winter camp, and constantly training and drilling, might not be such a bad life after all.

In March 1862 they finally received their long-awaited orders. The Brigade marched to boats that transported them to the Peninsula of Virginia, where they would become a part of the Union Peninsula Campaign. The Brigade arrived in bad weather. There was "no end to cold rain, sleet and mud. We had no fresh meat, no vegetables; nothing but fat pork, black coffee, and 'hard-tack' three times a day," wrote Father Corby. Moving into huts that had been occupied by Confederate soldiers during the winter, the Irish Brigade's first battle was waged against lice, which the soldiers called "graybacks." Father Corby recorded "incredible tortures" from the lice and felt that dealing with "this kind of life requires more courage than to face the belching cannon and the smoke of battle."

The Irish Brigade was soon involved in battling something more than camp hardships and lice. Father Corby and the other chaplains were busy after orders came on May 1st and the soldiers faced the prospect of real fighting ahead. "Our men confessed their sins, received Holy Communion, and spent their spare time in much serious reflection on the past and the very doubtful future, with its possibilities in the coming battle." The month of May saw the Irish Brigade marching through swamps, chasing a Confederate enemy that kept retreating before the Union army, drawing the Brigade

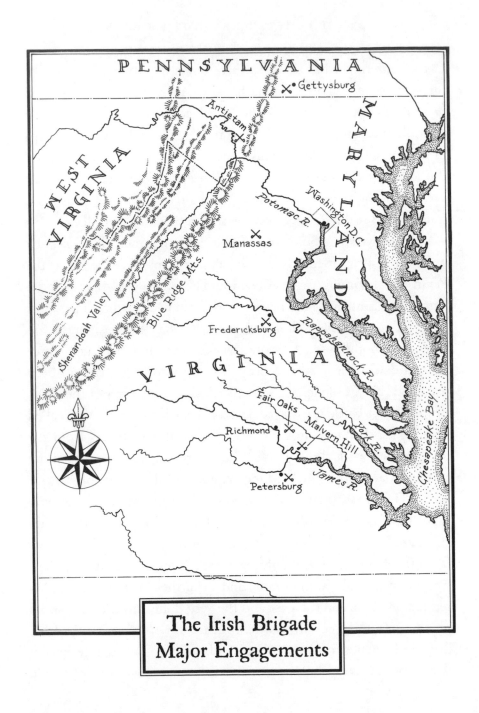

The Irish Brigade
Major Engagements

farther away from their supplies and exhausting the men. The first actual battle for the Irish Brigade wouldn't take place until June 1st when they finally met the enemy at Fair Oaks, Virginia.

The Union and Confederate armies had actually met on the Chickahominy River near Richmond, Virginia, two days before and the battle had begun on May 31st. The Irish Brigade could hear the "booming of the cannon" as they spent May 31st marching "through a swamp" that Captain Conyngham described as "deep, dark, and dismal, as desolate and dreary as the imagination could picture." June 1st found the brigade assigned to the front of the Union lines, and they "moved in the direction of the enemy with a bold defiant cheer." When the Confederates made one last effort to break through the Union lines, it was the Irish Brigade that "met them with fixed bayonets and a sweeping fire," which forced the Confederates back.

One observer of that battle wrote later of "the Irish Brigade in the glory of a fair, free fight." He wrote, "Other men go into fights finely, sternly, or indifferently, but the only man that really loves it, after all, is the green, immortal Irishman. So there, the brave lads from the old sod, with the chosen Meagher at their head, laughed, and fought, and joked, as if it were the finest fun in the world." This picture painted by Dr. Thomas Ellis, an army surgeon, is without doubt exaggerated, but there was no denying the fighting spirit of the Irish Brigade. The cost of their valor at Fair Oaks that day was about one hundred soldiers either killed or wounded. Father Corby remembered that there was no place to set up a hospital at Fair Oaks and so the wounded had to be placed in freight cars and sent back behind the lines to receive medical care. The transport made the men's suffering all the greater. Captain Conyngham saw Father Corby and the other chaplains that night "going through the battle-field, shriving the dying, and attending those who might recover," as they waited for transport to the hospitals.

The Irish Brigade had fought with great bravery and tenacity. Major General George B. McClellan, in command of all the Union forces on the Peninsula, came to General Meagher and asked him to tell his troops of "the gratification [I] feel at your steady valor and conduct at the battle of Fair Oaks." The Brigade remained in position on picket duty guarding the front lines, although they were not involved in any major battles over the next few weeks.

In late June the Irish Brigade was involved in the series of battles fought just outside of Richmond, Virginia, known as the Seven Days Battle. They were used as reserve troops, held back to be used only when most needed. Captain Conyngham recalled that when they would be finally called into action, "the dead, the wounded, the beaten, the broken and disheartened line our path—but our cheers reanimate—our *élan* gives them hope." In the final battle of the series, at Malvern Hill, the Irish Brigade sat out most of the fighting but were needed as the day ended. At their arrival on the field of battle, "stragglers, wounded, and retreating lines cheer on the Irish Brigade."

Vermont sharpshooter Brigham Buswell remembered the sight and sounds of the Irish Brigade's arrival on the field. McClellan "ordered Meagher's Irish Brigade to cross and charge the enemy back into the woods which they did with a series of those terrible yells for which this brigade was noted." Another writer described them also in terms of the noise they made—their "half-English, half-Gaelic battle cry that compared favorably with the dreaded Rebel yell."

The Irish Brigade quickly found themselves in a desperate situation "where hand-to-hand conflict ensues. Men brain and

Wounded soldiers being loaded onto trains for removal to hospitals during the Peninsula Campaign   *Library of Congress*

bayonet one another. The enemy make a bold stand to hold the hill, but in vain . . . McClellan's army is saved, but that hill-side is covered with the dying and dead of the Irish Brigade."

The Peninsula Campaign, as this whole series of battles in May and June of 1862 is known, was a stalemate. After some Union successes, Robert E. Lee was appointed the head of the Confederate army defending Richmond. Under his leadership, the Confederate Army of Northern Virginia became more aggressive in its attacks against the Union Army of the Potomac. General McClellan decided to withdraw the army rather than continue the fighting. General Lee repeatedly attacked the Union troops as they slowly pulled back from the outskirts of Richmond, but neither he nor General McClellan won a decisive victory in the series of bloody battles they fought. The only effect of the battles in this campaign were the 46,000 Union and Confederate casualties.

Seven hundred Irish soldiers were wounded or lay dead on the field by the conclusion of the Peninsula Campaign. In the retreat that followed, many of their dead and wounded had to be left behind. Captain Conyngham mourned some of the officers killed in the battle. He remembered Captain Joseph O'Donohoe, of Bantry, County Cork, aged twenty-two: "He had had so many escapes . . . and looked upon himself as one of the fortunate, who were fated to pass scathless through the fiery ordeal of war." After Manassas, he had found three holes in his clothing where bullets had passed through without touching him, but here at Malvern Hill, he "met a soldier's death." Lieutenant John H. Donovan "was shot through the right eye, the bullet going out through the ear just under the brain, and was left for dead." Amazingly, Lieutenant Donovan survived this normally mortal wound.

Charge of the 69th New York upon a Confederate battery, with the shamrock flag flying

General Meagher went home to New York to recruit replacements for his Brigade. Speaking to a group of Irishmen in New York in late July 1862, he listed the losses the Brigade had suffered in the Peninsula Campaign. The 69th was down to 295 from its 750 men of June 1st. The 88th had lost 200 men and had "just four hundred men fit for duty." The 63rd needed two hundred new recruits also. In his strongest oratorical style he called upon his fellow Irishmen "to throw themselves forward, and pledging themselves in life and death to it, to stand to the last by that noble little brigade which has been true to its military oath, true to the Republic... true to the memories, the pride and hopes of Ireland."

CHAPTER 8:

The Bloodiest Day

By the fall of 1862 Union President Abraham Lincoln desperately needed a decisive Union victory. The stalemate ending the Peninsula Campaign had been discouraging, especially after the rout of the Union army at Manassas the previous summer. There had been a second battle at Manassas in August 1862. Again the Union forces had been defeated. By now many Confederate leaders felt that victory for the South was only a battle away. They felt that it was time to take the war to the North. One more victory and the Confederacy was sure that other countries would recognize that they had earned their independence and acknowledge them as a separate nation. The Confederacy had everything to win by invading Union territory and moving the war to Northern soil.

Abraham Lincoln knew he had everything to lose if the Confederates were successful on Union soil. A Confederate victory in Maryland would leave the Union capital, Washington, sitting in the middle of Confederate territory. Maryland already had a high percentage of Southern supporters, especially in

Baltimore. A victory for the Confederates in Maryland could lead Maryland to secede and join the rest of the Southern states.

Lincoln also had a political reason for wanting a Union victory. He had finally made a decision to turn this war into a moral crusade. Lincoln had once said, "If I could save the Union without freeing any slave, I would do it; and if I could save it by freeing all the slaves, I would do it; and if I could do it by freeing some and leaving others alone, I would also do that." He now decided that it was time to turn this war into a fight over the evil of slavery. But he needed the right moment to issue his Emancipation Proclamation —he needed a Union victory.

In command of the Confederate Army of Northern Virginia, General Robert E. Lee had argued in favor of taking the war into Northern territory. His army had been trying to live off the land in Virginia. But with so much of Virginia either a battleground or disturbed by marching troops, food was becoming increasingly hard to find. Invading Maryland would give Lee and his army access to supplies and food in an area that hadn't been destroyed by the marching and fighting armies.

Lee and his army began crossing the Potomac River into Maryland on September 4, 1862. On September 8th, Lee issued a proclamation addressed "To the People of Maryland" in which he explained the presence of his army in their state. After listing all the actions taken by the Union government to suppress any support for the South in this border state, Lee wrote: "Our army has come among you, and is prepared to assist you with the power of its arms in regaining the rights of which you have been despoiled." The Confederate army would not force the citizens of Maryland to join them, he continued, but "the Southern people will rejoice to

The town of Sharpsburg in 1862   *Library of Congress*

welcome you to your natural position among them." To the Confederates' surprise, the vast majority of Marylanders did not respond to his plea. A few of them did come forward to offer aid and join the forces, but most stayed hidden in their homes and ignored the Confederate army. It was too late for Lee to turn back now. Although he would have liked the support of these people, he was confident of victory even if they opposed him.

Lee decided to divide his army. He sent General Thomas "Stonewall" Jackson to take possession of Harpers Ferry, Virginia (now West Virginia); General James Longstreet to the west, past South Mountain; and left the remainder of the army to guard his wagons and supplies in Maryland.

Meanwhile the Northern leaders were moving rapidly to prepare to repel this invasion. Major General McClellan, known as "Little Mac," had been replaced at the end of the Peninsula Campaign by Major General John Pope. After the second battle at Manassas, President Lincoln reappointed McClellan as army commander. McClellan moved quickly to reorganize the Army of the Potomac and get it into action to prevent Lee's army from advancing any farther north. The Union army (including the Irish Brigade) arrived at Frederick, Maryland, on September 12 just as the rear of the Confederate army was moving out.

General McClellan then had an incredible piece of luck. As the Union army moved into the camp on the Best Farm just south of Frederick that the Confederate army had just vacated, a Union soldier found a package with three cigars in it. As he opened the package, he saw that the paper the cigars were wrapped in had writing on it. This was not unusual since at that time most paper was used and reused until it wore out. But the message on this paper was

Sketch of the fighting in the Cornfield during the early part of the Battle of Antietam

unique. Written on it were General Lee's orders to his commanders —his entire plan for attacking the Union army, including where the three major parts of his army should be at different times! All General McClellan had to do was move fast and attack Lee's army while it was divided and before Lee found out that he knew his plans. McClellan himself is said to have exclaimed on reading the order: "Here is a paper with which if I cannot whip Bobbie Lee, I will be willing to go home."

General McClellan was well loved by his armies. He was a brilliant organizer and took good care of his soldiers. But Little Mac had one major fault that a successful general could not afford to have. He was too cautious. Instead of moving his army quickly, he delayed until the next day. Lee found out that McClellan knew of his plans from a Confederate sympathizer who had been at McClellan's headquarters when Little Mac was given the paper. The man slipped through Union lines, and by the evening of the day that the paper was found, Lee knew that he could not delay. He sent new orders for his commanders to finish up their current operations quickly and regroup. The Confederate armies converged on the little village of Sharpsburg, Maryland, near the banks of Antietam Creek. Lee would have to begin the fight without Stonewall Jackson and his men, who had just completed the capture of the Union garrison at Harpers Ferry, but he was confident that he could still defeat the Union army. Little Mac spent several days positioning his own army. There would be no fighting until September 17th. McClellan had totally lost any advantage he had gained when that soldier found the cigars wrapped in Lee's orders.

As the battle began on the morning of September 17th, the fighting was clustered around a wooded area and a cornfield. The

The Roulette farm, where the advance began to try to rout the Confederates from the Sunken Road   *Library of Congress*

Union troops left their protected position in the North Woods and attacked across a cornfield between two other wooded areas called the East and West Woods. The Union army was trying to break the left wing of the Confederate line, and they attacked over and over again. Bodies began to pile up in the cornfield. Confederate counterattacks just added rebel bodies to the bloody remains of the cornfield. When the leaders finally realized that neither side was going to break through at this end of the line, both armies stopped fighting. Losses were terrible on both sides. One Union division of about 3,000 soldiers lost half of its men in twenty minutes of fighting. One Confederate unit of about 550 soldiers lost 323 in the fighting in the cornfield.

As the area around the cornfield and woods grew quiet, another part of the battle was already underway a little farther south, toward the center of the battle lines. Three Confederate brigades had taken over a small depression called the Sunken Road at the edge of a local farm owned by the Roulette family. It gave them a wonderful defensive position. Any troops that tried to attack had to come across an open field and up a rise. The Confederates could simply pick them off as they topped the rise. For a Union victory, it was essential that the army drive out these rebels holding the Sunken Road. Several attempts had already been made and had failed. But there was one brigade that was a natural to lead the new attack—the Irish Brigade.

This picture of Bloody Lane today shows why it was such a natural defensive position for the Confederates, and also why they would be trapped if Union troops got to their flank, or side, which is where this picture is sighted.

W. Michael Beller

CHAPTER 9:

Heroes of Bloody Lane

"**The** rebels seemed to have a special spite against the green flag, and five color-bearers were shot down successively in a short time. As the last man fell even these Irishmen hesitated a moment to assume a task synonymous with death. 'Big Gleason,' Captain of the 63rd New York, six feet seven, sprang forward and snatched it up. In a few minutes a bullet struck the staff, shattering it to pieces; Gleason tore the flag from the broken staff, wrapped it around his body, putting his sword-belt over it, and went through the rest of that fight untouched," wrote Meagher's biographer, Michael Cavanagh.

The Irish Brigade was fearless as the soldiers attempted the impossible task of dislodging the determined Confederates from the Sunken Road. As orders came to attack, Chaplain Corby "told the men to make an Act of Contrition. As they were coming toward me...I only had time to wheel my horse for an instant toward them and gave my poor men a hearty absolution...In twenty or thirty minutes after this absolution, 506 of these very men lay on the field, either dead or seriously wounded."

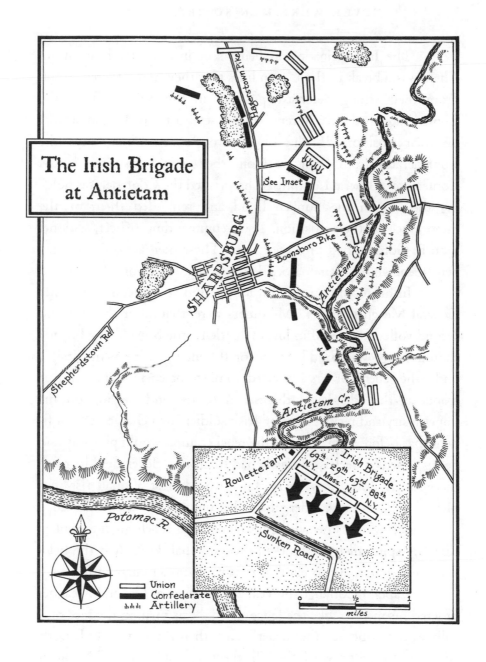

The Irish Brigade
at Antietam

See Inset

Hagerstown Pike

SHARPSBURG

Boonsboro Pike

Antietam Cr.

Shepherdstown Rd.

Antietam Cr.

Potomac R.

Roulette Farm · Irish Brigade

69th 29th 63rd 88th
N.Y. Mass. N.Y. N.Y.

Sunken Road

Union
Confederate
Artillery

0   ½   1
miles

The Irish Brigade was being sent into a terrible position. There was a break in the Union lines that they were ordered to fill. From their strong defensive position in the Sunken Road the Confederates had already repulsed the several major Union attacks on their position. If the Union troops could not drive the Confederates from their position, they would lose the battle. Confederate General Lee himself had visited the Confederates holding the line in the Sunken Road and reminded them of the importance of their position. Their commanding officer, Colonel John B. Gordon, had promised Lee: "These men are going to stay here, General, till the sun goes down or victory is won."

In his report on the Brigade's action at Antietam, Brigadier General Meagher wrote: "My orders were, that, after the first and second volleys delivered in line of battle by the brigade, the brigade should charge with fixed bayonets on the enemy... It was my design, under the general orders I received, to push the enemy on both their fronts as they displayed themselves to us, and, relying on the impetuosity and recklessness of Irish soldiers in a charge, felt confident that before such a charge the rebel column would give way and be dispersed." The Irish Brigade had to cross a clover field to reach the enemy, "300 paces" away. They would crest a small rise in a plowed field, and it was here that other units before them had failed to advance against the withering fire of the rebels in the Sunken Road. A split-rail fence blocked their way halfway across the field, and they would have to climb over it while under enemy fire.

Captain Conyngham recalled the scene as General Meagher ordered his men to take the fence down: "His men, in the face of a galling fire, obeyed the order" and then "the whole Brigade advanced to the brow of the hill, cheering as they went." Meagher noted their excitement in his report: "Never did men with such alacrity and generosity of heart press forward and encounter the perils of the battle-field."

"Gallowglass," the pen name of James Turner on Meagher's staff, wrote an account of this courageous charge of the Irish Brigade for *The Irish American*: "The Brigade soon came within range of the enemy's small arms. The advance ... was uninterrupted, unbroken although it had to be made under many difficulties, the chief of which was the close, compact, and strong fences, which impeded the progress of the men ... All this time the bullets were whirring about ... The fire as we mount the slope is terrific but the advance never falters or wavers ... the Brigade pushes up the hill slowly, steadily, surely, pouring into the ranks of the enemy a deadly and telling fire."

Captain Conyngham recalled General Meagher, rallying his brigade, "Boys, raise the colors, and follow me!" General McClellan watched the fighting from a hilltop. As the flag-bearers were shot down, the Irish Brigade's flag fell over and over again. One of McClellan's aides thought the Irish were lost and would have to retreat. McClellan "looked on for a moment, and smilingly replied—'No, no! their flags are up— they are charging!'" The Irish Brigade fought its way onward nearer and nearer to the Sunken Road. Captain Conyngham wrote that the firing was so intense that "the muskets were become red-hot in men's hands ...The men had often to fling away their muskets, and pick others up." Many others were available from the dead soldiers, who needed theirs no more. Meagher's report noted that the fire of the Confederate soldiers in the Sunken Road "literally cut lanes through our approaching line." Meagher's biographer, Michael Cavanagh, later wrote that "the

Dead Confederate soldiers in the Sunken Road. Notice the vegetation chopped off by the intense musket and cannon fire.   *Library of Congress*

colors were shot down sixteen times, and on each occasion a man was ready to spring forward and place the colors in front." Several of the officers had horses shot out from under them. General Meagher's "clothes were perforated with bullets," wrote Captain Conyngham.

The Irish Brigade fought its way to within "30 paces" of the Sunken Road but could go no further. They maintained their position until they ran out of ammunition. Other units could not reach them through the terrible gunfire across the field. Finally, ammunition exhausted, the Irish Brigade had no choice but to move back across the field. This would not be the disorderly retreat of a defeated unit, however. To the amazement of everyone who witnessed it, the members of the Brigade stood up and, "Forming in columns of four, at the right shoulder shift," left the field in regular formation. Noted one historian, "the shot up regiments defied the incoming Confederate rounds and prepared to leave the field with a professional arrogance."

It would take fresh Union troops approaching the Sunken Road from the side and firing into the flanks of the Confederate troops to finally capture their position and end the fighting in this road known now as Bloody Lane. Union Brigadier General D. H. Strother described the scene as he looked down at the Sunken Road. He wrote: "I could easily distinguish the movements of those endeavoring to crawl away from the ground; hands waving as if calling of assistance, and others struggling as if in the agonies of death." The photographs that were taken after the battle in Bloody Lane were the first photographs ever taken of battlefield dead. They shocked the world. The bodies lay piled several layers deep along the whole length of Bloody Lane. Eyewitnesses confirmed what the photographs showed—a person could walk the length of Bloody

Lane and never touch ground. As for the Irish Brigade, many of their soldiers and officers remained "30 paces" from the Sunken Road, dead or dying. Wrote one historian of the Irish Brigade's fight at Antietam: "The dogged bravery of the Irish had never been questioned, and the brigade's action at Antietam fully sustained its reputation for utter bravery in the face of fire."

Bloody Lane today, photographed from the same angle as in the preceding photograph, while standing in the depression that was covered by dead soldiers.

CHAPTER 10:

Dead Irishmen

"Captain John Kavanagh is no more. Fighting for liberty, fighting for his adopted country, the gallant fellow has fallen. As true an Irishman—as loyal, as brave an American citizen as ever breathed the breath of life, lies in strange earth to-day." The obituary for Kavanagh, which appeared in the New York paper *The Irish American*, was full of anguish for this Irish hero who had stood with Meagher and Young Ireland in 1848.

He died defending his new home, and *The Irish American* remembered him: "He was comparatively a young man, less than thirty-seven years of age; of medium height; slender, but sinewy frame; fair complexion; and of prompt, decisive mental habits. He has left a wife and seven children…He was a most energetic and fearless officer. He fell at the head of his company, in the heat of action."

September 17, 1862, had been a glorious but awful day for the Irish Brigade. They had paid a terrible price for their courageous advance at Bloody Lane. *The Irish American* put the toll for the 69th New York at 36 killed, 164 wounded, and 2 missing. Their own

Union soldiers burying the dead from Bloody Lane

correspondent, writing as "Gallowglass," had been wounded in the fighting. He wrote the newspaper a personal letter, telling of the battle and the carnage that followed. *The Irish American* printed the letter in full as a news article.

"Gallowglass" described the aftermath of the fight:

> Yesterday wet and dreary as the dull day was, they bore [Captain John O'Connell] Joyce and Kavanagh and laid them in the damp earth of Calvary; a day or two ago they carried [Captain Felix] Duffy to the house that lasts till doomsday; [Captain Patrick F.] Clooney lies on some hill-side in Maryland, not far, I suppose, from the spot where he fell; the unnamed heroes who charged, up that hill-side, the rebel flags planted on top of it, and the rebel bullets almost darkening the sunlight and showering down its slope, are buried not far from the battle-field; they fill soldiers' graves every one of them, and the least we can do is to seize their names even for a day from the dark oblivion into which they have fallen.

Captain John O'Connell Joyce was born in Fermoy, Ireland. His obituary notes that "While leading his men bravely against the foe, he fell, shot through the head, dying instantly." Captain Patrick F. Clooney had only come from Ireland in 1861 and had immediately enlisted in the Irish Brigade. *The Irish American* described his valor at Bloody Lane: "On the battle-field of Antietam his commanding form could be seen remarkably conspicuous among his comrades. High above the din of battle, his rich, manly voice could be heard encouraging his men and inspiring them to action... After receiving a gun-shot

Union burial detail working near the Cornfield area of the battlefield

wound in the knee, he would not leave the field … No he kept his place, until a rifle bullet passed through his body, killing him instantly."

"Gallowglass" further described the scene: "Captain Clooney receives a bullet through the knee: the pain is torturing, terrible … he seizes the colors and hobbles along on one leg … two musket balls strike him; one enters his brain, the other his heart, and he falls dead." Captain Conyngham remembered the death of Captain Duffy, "one of the most dashing officers in the Brigade."

There were other similar accounts of the deaths of the brave officers of the Irish Brigade: "Captain Miller had his horse shot under him … [Meagher's] horse is shot, falls heavily on the rider, who is taken up insensible." Carried to the rear of the lines, Meagher was fine in spite of the fact that his "clothes were perforated with bullets." Captain D. S. Shanley had been wounded at Malvern Hill in June, but was back with the brigade for the fight at Antietam. He died at Antietam "while bravely leading on his company." Lieutenant R. A. Kelly, a native of Athy, County Kildare, was "a splendid specimen of manhood, being, though only twenty-one years of age, fully six feet three inches in height," in the words of Captain Conyngham. He had been wounded while fighting with the 69th at Manassas, but that did not prevent him from being one of the first to enlist in the Irish Brigade. Conyngham wrote that "no better soldier fell on the bloody plain of Antietam."

There were also those who had been wounded. Captain Jasper Whitty, wounded at Manassas, lost an eye at White Oak Swamp and was now wounded again at Antietam. He resigned, his injuries finally too severe for him to fight again. Captain Michael O'Sullivan, of Dublin, who "served with distinction through the different battles until that of Antietam, when he was wounded in the

A barn being used as a hospital after the Battle of Antietam

knee by a rifle-ball," also resigned "in consequence of his wounds."

The official report of casualties for the Irish Brigade at the Battle of Antietam for the three main regiments of the Brigade (the 69th, 63rd, and 88th New York Volunteers) listed 11 officers killed along with 97 enlisted men. Fourteen officers were wounded along with 384 enlisted men. It was the Brigade's bloodiest day. Of the 2,944 men who began the fight, 506 lay wounded or dead on the field. The Brigade would go on to fight again, but the losses sustained in the fight for Bloody Lane could never be made up.

CHAPTER 11:

Heroes Yet Again—the Brigade at Fredericksburg

The Irish Brigade did fight again just three months later at Fredericksburg, Virginia, on December 13, 1862. Their fierce reputation preceded them this time. Watching them move into position to charge Marye's Heights, Confederate General D. H. Hill commented, "There are those damned green flags again."

The assault on Marye's Heights at Fredericksburg was an almost hopeless task, which is probably why the Irish Brigade was ordered to perform it. The Confederates were well positioned on a steep ridge behind a stone wall. They could pour fire on any attackers while being protected from return fire. Meagher knew that he was leading his men into near certain death and, ever true to Ireland, he gave them the motivation they would need: "Meagher resolved his men should carry the 'colors of their Fatherland' into what promised to be the bloodiest fight ... [he] ordered a sprig of evergreen be placed in each soldier and officer's cap, himself setting the example." Then he urged them on to victory: "I know this day you will strike a deadly blow to those wicked traitors who are now but a few hundred yards from you, and bring back to this distracted country its former prestige and glory."

But victory was not to be for the Union armies that day. The Irish Brigade could not save the day. *The Times of London*, rare in its praise of the Irish, was awed by their actions on Marye's Heights. "Never...was a more undaunted courage displayed by the sons of Erin than during those six frantic dashes which they directed against the almost impregnable position of the foe."

Chaplain William Corby watched as the Brigade was almost destroyed: "The place into which Meagher's brigade was sent was simply a slaughter-pen...Our brigade was cut to pieces...We had only the remnant of a brigade." Captain Conyngham wrote a vivid description of the horrors of the charges as the Irish Brigade advanced to "within sixty yards of the enemy's batteries, and are met by a most disastrous enfilade and direct fire from the rebel artillery and infantry...It was not a battle—it was a wholesale slaughter of human beings." The Irish Brigade advanced further than any other unit in the charge and at times "the advance of the Brigade was actually impeded by the bodies piled upon one another."

Captain Conyngham reported that "two-thirds of the officers and men of the Brigade are lying on that bloody field." Conyngham quotes from a letter sent home by one of the surviving Irish officers: "As for the Brigade, may the Lord pity and protect the widows and orphans of nearly all of those belonging to it! It will be a sad, sad Christmas by many an Irish hearthstone." Meagher's official report gave the numbers: "Of the one thousand two hundred I led into action the day before, two hundred and eighty only appeared."

Color Sergeant Peter Welsh of the 28th Massachusetts wrote to his wife on December 18, 1862: "thank God i came out

The Stone Wall at Fredericksburg, site of the Irish Brigade's heroic but deadly charge

of it safe it was a fierce and bloody battle our brigade got teribly cut up it is so small now that it is not fit to go into any further action unless it is recruited up."

Captain Conyngham provided an account of the Irish Brigade's strength and casualties throughout the course of their service with the Army of the Potomac. He gave the total strength of the three original units of the Brigade as 2,944 men. By the end of the war, he recorded 1,352 of these as killed, wounded, or missing. The Brigade's worst day was at Antietam, when there were 506 casualties. After the charge on Marye's Heights, another 296 of the already weakened unit had become casualties. It must indeed have been a "sad, sad Christmas by many an Irish hearthstone."

Some Irish Brigade officers in camp at Fredericksburg, including Father Corby, sitting on the right

CHAPTER 12:

On and On—
the Legend Continues

In some ways, after Fredericksburg, the Irish Brigade would never be the same. In other ways, the story would just go on and on. The legend of the Irish Brigade is made up of more than just the bravery of the soldiers who fought in it. The Brigade also brought to the army a fiery spirit and a playfulness and love of life that was renowned throughout the Union army. It wasn't just for what they did on the battlefield that they are remembered, but also for their St. Patrick's Day celebrations, their races, and their music. What happened at the Irish Brigade's St. Patrick's Day celebration of 1863 is a good example of the Irish spirit they brought to army life during the Civil War. After all the losses they had sustained in the fighting in 1862, one would expect to find the unit demoralized. But not the Irish Brigade.

March 17, 1863, began with Mass, held in a church built in the woods for just this day's services. The services were attended not just by members of the Irish Brigade but also by General Hooker, commander in chief of the Army of the Potomac, and members of his staff.

The Irish Brigade celebrates St. Patrick's Day in 1863, sketched by Edwin Forbes, an artist who traveled with the armies during the Civil War.

Library of Congress

"After the morning's religious devotions came the sports," wrote Chaplain Corby. "...It was estimated at the time that fully twenty thousand participated in, or at least witnessed the sports of the day." After the horse races, which "far surpassed the expectations of the multitude," lunch was served "under the extensive bower, constructed of pine branches...Ham sandwiches, lemonade and other delicacies were prepared there, and probably not less than fifteen hundred partook of the generous hospitality of Gen. Meagher and the Irish Brigade," wrote Corby. The day continued with all sorts of individual contests—footraces, throwing weights, sack races, hurdle jumping, and others, all with generous prizes for the winners. At the end of the day, the party still continued, "followed by a grand entertainment at night, theatricals and recitations," remembered Captain Conyngham. Captain Conyngham also took note of the appreciation of General Hooker and their other guests for the Irish Brigade's "spiced whiskey-punch."

The Irish brought to the army the "exhaustless spirit and enthusiasm of Irish nature," wrote Captain Conyngham. The soldiers who formed the Brigade earned both their reputations for fearlessness and their reputations for memorable parties and celebrations that "drew the admiration of the entire Army of the Potomac," remembered Father Corby. In the midst of all the death that the Civil War brought, they could still find time to celebrate life and give thanks to their Irish patron saint before returning to the fight.

At Chancellorsville in May 1863, with the opening of the spring campaign, the Brigade suffered another sixty-four casualties. Early in the battle, the small Irish Brigade was not engaged in the actual fighting. Instead, they were left to guard fords across the Rappahannock River near Fredericksburg, Virginia, to protect

The steeplechase races at the Irish Brigade's St. Patrick's Day celebration, sketched by Edwin Forbes   *Library of Congress*

the rear of the Union army from a surprise Confederate attack.

Then, on Sunday morning, May 3rd, the Irish Brigade was ordered to the front lines to support the Fifth Maine Battery, which was under severe attack by the Confederates. Captain Conyngham remembered their march to the front: "As we marched through the woods, shot and shell were poured like hail upon us." They arrived just as the Union battery was giving way under heavy fire, and in Captain Conygham's words, "did good service to the Union." Advancing across the field, the brigade was able to hold back the Confederates just long enough to gain time for the guns of the battery to be saved. But as always, there was a price to be paid for the soldiers' courage and gallantry. Captain Conyngham vividly remembered two incidents from the action. "Here Captain Lynch was killed, being cut right through the centre with a solid shot." The second incident was a personal one, as "a shell burst right in front of me. Fortunately there was another officer just before me, who got the whole contents of it."

With the added losses at Chancellorsville, Meagher knew that there was no way to recruit enough men to fill the ranks of the Irish Brigade, now reduced to fewer than five hundred able-bodied soldiers. Meagher requested permission to temporarily remove the Brigade from the army and allow it time to rebuild. But his request was turned down by the Union army high command because they felt the unit could not be spared. In disgust, Meagher resigned from his position of leadership of the Irish Brigade.

Retiring Brigadier General Meagher addressed his soldiers for the last time on May 19, 1863, praising them for the outstanding reputation they had earned for the Irish Brigade. He told them that their "sacrifices ... [had] made its history ... sacred and inestimable." In an emotional farewell, he spoke of "the graves of many hundreds of brave and devoted soldiers, who went to death with all the radiance and enthusiasm of the noblest chivalry." Then with cheers and "many a manly eye ... filled with tears," he turned over his command.

Command of the remaining members of the Irish Brigade was given to Colonel Robert Nugent. An Irishman from Kilkeel, County Down, Nugent had been with the Brigade since the beginning. Wounded at Fredericksburg, he now brought his "high executive ability and undoubted gallantry" to the command of the legendary Irish Brigade.

The Irish Brigade participated in an assault made by the Second Corps at Gettysburg, Pennsylvania, on July 2, 1863. They were successful in forcing back the Confederates, who threatened to overrun a critical part of the Union line on Cemetery Ridge. But the Irish Brigade would be remembered more that day for the actions of only one of its members. As the Brigade prepared to move into battle, Chaplain Corby had a major concern. The soldiers "had had absolutely no chance to practise their religious duties during the past two or three weeks, being constantly on the march." Knowing that many of the men standing there would die, he could not allow them to go to their deaths without giving them a chance to confess their sins before "cannon from their [Confederate] side belched forth from their fiery throats missiles of death into our lines." Colonel St. Clair Mulholland of the Irish Brigade described what happened next: "Father Corby stood on a large rock in front of the brigade. Addressing the men ... saying each one could receive the benefit of absolution ... and reminding them of the high and sacred nature of their trust as soldiers ... As he closed his address, every man, Catholic and non-Catholic, fell on his knees with his head bowed down." Chaplain Corby thought he was ministering only to his own men, but as large groups of Union soldiers of all religions knelt in prayer, the moment became "more than impressive; it was awe-inspiring," in the words of Colonel Mulholland. Father Corby himself was moved as "even Maj.-Gen. Hancock [Commander of the Union 2nd Army Corps] removed his hat ... and bowed in reverential devotion." As he looked back on the day, Father Corby reflected: "That general absolution was intended for all ... not only for our brigade, but for all, North or South ... who were about to appear before their Judge." Another Union officer watching would remember that scene as "one of the most picturesque and beautiful incidents" of the Civil War. Today a statue of Father Corby stands near the spot at Gettysburg where he gave absolution to the soldiers.

The fighting at Gettysburg added yet another seventy-five names to the list of the Irish Brigade casualties. In late 1863, the Irish Brigade veterans who had reenlisted had a chance to return home to New York for a short furlough. Colonel Nugent spent that time trying to rebuild the Brigade. The recruitment of several new companies of men and the addition of the 28th Massachusetts and 116th Pennsylvania Volunteers to the original New York regiments brought the Brigade up to the minimum number of troops required to remain a brigade.

As fighting began again in May 1864, the replenished Irish Brigade was ready. The fighting at the battles for the Wilderness and Spotsylvania Court House, close by Fredericksburg, Virginia, where they had already fought twice before, found the Brigade fighting side by side with the Corcoran Legion, another New York unit made up

Statue of Father Corby at Gettysburg marks the spot where he blessed the troops before they went into battle. *W. Michael Beller*

mostly of Irish-Americans, with both units losing several officers and many men in the long and bitter fighting. As General Grant's bloody advance on Richmond continued, the Brigade and the legion added to the considerable fighting reputation of the Irish soldier when they together charged a hill at Cold Harbor, Virginia, on June 3, 1864, "holding a position on the crest for two hours, against fearful odds."

Moving on to Petersburg, Virginia, the Irish Brigade ended up "in a place where a converging fire decimated its ranks." Less than six months after being "recruited up" to brigade strength again, the Irish Brigade had lost "one thousand men and officers, or one-third of its entire strength, in killed, wounded, or missing." And so it would continue until the following spring. General Nugent would recruit men, but the war would use them up almost faster than he could recruit them.

In September 1864 the Irish Brigade celebrated their third anniversary in camp near Petersburg. One of the guests of honor was Thomas Francis Meagher. Addressing the assembled men of the brigade, who had been given the day off from duty to celebrate, Meagher reminded them of their proud Irish heritage. He told them that "they had proved themselves worthy descendants of their fore-fathers, both in valor and patriotism ... no other country had contributed so much to the honor of the flag of America as Ireland."

CHAPTER 13:

Lost Dreams

The war between the states finally came to an end. The Union's long siege of Richmond and Petersburg was finally successful in April of 1865. The Union Army of the Potomac and the smaller Army of the James chased the remnants of Lee's proud Confederate Army of Northern Virginia to Appomattox Court House, Virginia, where they were cut off from their supplies and surrounded. There, in a farmhouse parlor, Confederate General Robert E. Lee and Union General Ulysses S. Grant met to bring the fighting to an end. Although other smaller units of the Confederate armies would continue fighting for several more weeks, General Lee surrendered on April 9, 1865, and the war was effectively over.

By the end of the war, most soldiers wanted to go home and forget what they had been through. The remaining soldiers of the Irish Brigade marched in the grand review of the troops in Washington, D.C., on May 23, 1865, in front of "an immense concourse of citizens from all parts of the country," wrote Irish Brigade Surgeon William O'Meagher. The Brigade went home to New York, where they were part of a momentous Fourth of July celebration and then were mustered out of service.

Thomas Francis Meagher was also mustered out of the army. His resignation was accepted on May 15, 1865. Not quite sure what he wanted to do now that the war was over, Meagher did what many other Civil War soldiers did. He headed west. Arriving in St. Paul, Minnesota, on July 23rd, he was greeted as the hero of the Irish Brigade. He continued on his way to Montana, where he served as Acting Governor of the Montana Territory. The Western Territories were wild and untamed at this point in history, and it would have been very difficult for anyone to govern them effectively. Meagher's time as acting governor was marked by much controversy. Some of it came from people who did not want to see the rule of law established in the territory. But some of the controversy came from Meagher himself. He was used to giving orders and having them obeyed and was not a very patient governor. Meagher would not be in Montana for long. Traveling to meet a ship arriving at Fort Benton, Meagher became ill. Arriving at Fort Benton on July 1, 1867, a friend (and fellow Irishman) invited him to spend the night on his ship. Meagher was delirious with fever and, at some point during the night, forgetting where he was, left his room and fell off the ship into the Missouri River and drowned. His body was never found. It was a tragic end for this hero of the Young Ireland Rebellion and the Irish Brigade.

The soldiers of the Irish Brigade returning to civilian life were now seasoned veterans of combat. Throughout the war a group called the Fenian Brotherhood, who were the Irish-American leaders urging a military takeover in Ireland, kept planning for their coming war with England. As the Civil War came to an end and all these trained soldiers became available, the time to act on their plans had arrived.

Some Irish-American veterans did go over to Ireland to train the Irish there. Since they made no attempt to hide what they were doing, they were quickly taken prisoner by the police. Another group of Irish-American veterans attempted an attack on Canada, which was part of the British empire. They hoped to hold it "hostage" to gain Irish independence. But the Irish in Canada did not rise up to help with the takeover. Although there was much vocal support among the Irish-American veterans for helping in a fight for Irish independence, no one ever organized them enough to achieve any real activity.

The Fenian dream, which Meagher had supported, of having the Irish Civil War veterans use their military experience to free Ireland from the British by force was doomed to failure. With the Irish-American veterans' emotional support for Ireland, it might seem surprising that when the time came the planned action never took place. It is true that if the Fenian leaders had been much better organized, they might have been able to raise a strong group of Irish veterans to help launch a revolution. But the failure was due to more than that. The Irish who went off to fight in the Civil War were changed by their experience. Somewhere along the way during the course of the war, the Irish had become Americans.

The Irish veterans were heroes. They had shared a horrible experience with all of the other immigrants who had come to America before them. By their bravery and with their blood they proved that they belonged to this new country. Irish Brigade historian Paul Jones wrote that the brigade's "proud record in the Civil War...helped to change the nation's pattern of thinking about

Requiem Mass in St. Patrick's Cathedral, New York City, for the
dead soldiers of the Irish Brigade. *Library of Congress*

Irish emigrants ... no one who saw the Brigade go into battle against all odds could have any doubt of the Irish-American's rights to full citizenship."

The Irish and the Irish Brigade had earned for themselves a very special place in the hearts of their fellow Americans. As Father Corby wrote in his memoirs, "One good result of the Civil War was the removing of a great amount of prejudice. When men stand in common danger, a fraternal feeling springs up between them."

The Irish Brigade had earned a place in history for all of the Irish-Americans who came to America to begin a new life. Irish soldiers lay buried throughout the North and South. Some, like those bodies found in 1988 in a farmer's field, lay in unmarked and long-forgotten battlefield graves. The Irish dead left behind them a vivid image in the American memory. Those who fought with them and those who fought against them could never forget their spirit and courage.

Confederate General Robert E. Lee, whose soldiers faced the Irish Brigade in battle so many times over the long years of fighting, gave the Irish-American soldiers their highest accolade after the war: "the Irish soldier fights not so much for lucre as through the reckless love of adventure ... the gallant stand which his [Meagher's] bold brigade made on the heights of Fredericksburg is well known. Never were men so brave. They ennobled their race by their splendid gallantry."

On a battlefield covered with white marble monuments, the Irish Brigade monument at Gettysburg stands out. The Celtic cross is made of green Connemara marble brought from Ireland. Even in marking death, the Irish Brigade survivors remembered Ireland. *W. Michael Beller*

SOURCES FOR
RESEARCH

Abodaher, David J. *Rebel on Two Continents: Thomas Meagher.* New York: J. Messner, 1970.

Athearn, Robert G. *Thomas Francis Meagher: An Irish Revolutionary in America.* New York: Arno Press, 1976.

Cavanagh, Michael. *Memoirs of Gen. Thomas Francis Meagher.* Worcester, Massachusetts: The Messenger Press, 1892.

Conyngham, David Power. *The Irish Brigade and Its Campaigns.* New York: William McSorley & Co., 1867.

Corby, William. *Memoirs of Chaplain Life: Three Years with the Irish Brigade in the Army of the Potomac.* Notre Dame, Indiana: Scholastic Press, 1894.

Frassanito, William A. *Antietam: The Photographic Legacy of America's Bloodiest Day.* New York: Charles Scribner's Sons, 1978.

A History of Kilmainham Gaol. Dublin: Office of Public Works, 1995.

The Irish American. New York, February 1, 1862–February 10, 1866. Bound volume. Periodicals Division, Library of Congress, Washington, D.C.

Irish News. New York, 1856–1861. Bound volume. Periodicals Division, Library of Congress, Washington, D.C.

Jones, Paul. *The Irish Brigade.* Washington, D.C.: Robert B. Luce, Inc., 1969.

Lyons, W. F. *Brigadier General Thomas Francis Meagher: His political and military career.* New York: D & J Sadlier, 1870.

Mitchel, John. *Jail Journal*. Glasgow: Cameron & Ferguson, 1876.

Priest, John Michael. *Antietam: The Soldiers' Battle*. New York: Oxford University Press, 1989.

Sears, Stephen W. *The Landscape Turned Red*. New York: Warner Books, 1983.

The Times of London. 1848. On Microfilm in the Periodicals Division, Library of Congress, Washington, D.C.

War of the Rebellion: A Compilation of the Official Records of the Union and Confederate Armies. Washington, D.C.: Government Printing Office, 1889.

Welsh, Peter. *Irish Green and Union Blue*. New York: Fordham University Press, 1986.

Woodham-Smith, Cecil. *The Great Hunger: Ireland 1845–1849*. New York: Harper & Row, 1962.

INDEX